CHRISTOPHER
and the
SWORDSMAN

How the Christ-Child
and the Music Was Saved

MARK J. WELCH

Cover design by Sophia Welch with additional help from Mark Ranet.

Also, Thanks to Ken Gould for helping to keep my head in the game.

Christopher and the Swordsman

How the Christ-Child and the Music Was Saved

Hard cover ISBN: 978-1-66788-226-0

eBook ISBN: 978-1-66788-227-7

For He shall give His
angels charge over you,
to keep you in all your ways.

—PSALM 91, VERSE 11

Dedication

In Memoriam

I have lost many friends and loved ones.

Too many to mention,

but I would like to mention one:

CHRISTOPHER KNOX PRICE

This is for you, Chris.

CONTENTS

"Music has been called the speech of angels;

I will go further,

and call it the speech of God himself."

—CHARLES KINGSLEY

CHAPTER 1:

A LIGHT IN THE DARK

Chris had just said good night to his dad after practicing his drums "a little too loud and a little too late", according to Dad. There had been some good-natured kidding about a new set of drums, but they both knew that any new purchases would not be an option for a while. Since his mother had died, it was hard for Dad to hold a job. Chris was now toying with the idea of quitting his drumming gigs and taking a job to help his dad. Chris had a gift for music, but he loved the drums. He was good. And when he played, everyone knew he was good, confident, sure of himself. There was a kind of primal power about drums, and he felt it throughout his body when he played. The striking of a drum released an ancient energy. It moved through the body like electricity through a thundercloud. It was in his blood, his heartbeat, and the rhythm of his breathing, a tonal vibration so deep and so basic that it was felt rather than heard. It was the roll of distant thunder, but up close and personal. That feeling is something not many young men have, and he was thinking about giving up that feeling to help his dad.

Chris had been in bed just a few minutes and had reached that in-between time of sleep and wakefulness. *Click.* The lamp beside his bed came on by itself. Chris, without even thinking about it, without opening his eyes, leaned over to the nightstand and clicked off the light. Some time went by. *Click.* The light came on again. This time something registered, but just barely. He opened his eyes, saw the figure at the foot of the bed, then leaned over to the nightstand, clicked off the light, punched his pillow twice, and closed his eyes.

"Wait for it," he heard or thought he heard, or *was it in his head?*

Click.

"Third time is the charm," said the figure at the foot of the bed. This time, it was Chris who turned on the light. He looked at the figure at the foot of the bed. He blinked. He looked again. There was a pause while Chris sucked in a fair amount of air before yelling out that word. A noun, actually, that every boy all over the world has cried out a million, billion times since there have been fathers and sons, a single-syllable word that means Help, What now?!, Get out!, Thank God you're here!, and everything around and in-between (depending, of course, on the occasion and inflection of the voice): "Daaaaaaddddddd!!!!" In this case, it was a cry for help. In the ensuing payhem (panic and mayhem), there were many questions and answers and calming down of panic, more questions and answers, and reassurances, and moderation of mayhem, followed by yet more questions and attempts at explanations, and eventual realization or, perhaps revelation that, for some things in this world there are no logical explanations. But, however strange, an explanation was required. Included in this explanation was a re-affirmation that neither Chris, nor his father would come to harm.

"You know this to be true," chided Michael, "for if you do not know me, your inner voice, that which is your soul, is well acquainted with me and is in fact glad to be reunited with one from the Light. You must trust me, Chris, for without trust there can be no truth. Without truth, your story will remain untold, your questions unanswered.

"Ok" said Chris. Though confused, he had to admit to himself that he really didn't feel threatened by…"My name is Michael."…anymore, and he did have questions.

Michael began slowly. He couldn't give it all away all at once. After all, this boy was only human. Indeed, he was well acquainted with this human. Together they had fought against a great darkness. A debt long overdue must now be paid.

"This thing you are going to do; stop your music, get a job,…is…"

"Look," Chris began, rolling his eyes, "I live in the real world. Here, we need to eat, keep a roof over our heads, and make sacrifices. You know about sacrifices, don't you?"

Michael tried to think of something he could say. Whatever decision Chris made had to be his own. The act of influencing another was a tricky business. "Please continue," was all he could think of for the moment.

"…Yeah. Well, Dad needs help, and even if I could get a steady gig, they don't pay enough. I couldn't make enough money. It's time I faced up to the fact that no one cares that much about music anymore, if they ever did."

"Are you quite sure that you feel that way?" asked Michael.

Chris just nodded, looking down at the floor.

"You are a Musician," Michael began. "You play the keyboard, guitar,…"

"…and drums," Chris finished, "…and I sing, too."

"Yes!" said Michael. "You play several instruments! You are gifted, blessed!"

"Mmmm, I certainly don't feel blessed," said Chris.

"Trust me," said Michael. "You are blessed."

Chris swallowed hard and looked up at Michael. "Yeah?" he asked.

"Yes," said Michael.

Chris shook his head. He didn't want to go into how many adults had told him he could not make a living in music. "I don't know. It just seems like…like…"

"No one cares," Michael finished.

"You do not feel valued. You feel…unappreciated,"

"Well, yeah! Definitely!" Chris agreed, but he wasn't quite ready to get too enthusiastic.

"Let me tell you how it should be here, and how it is in my world," said Michael.

"Okay," said Chris, brightening up a little. "Fine, tell me how it is, how it should be…or…whatever." He was still skeptical. Michael put his hands together as if to pray and looked at Chris. He thought back centuries, eons ago, when man had not yet come and there were only his kind, the universe, the Word, and the Music. Then he thought of how the Music was lost and about the prophecy, and the return of the Music, and the sacrifice it took. But *No, come back to the present. Come back to now.* It took only an instant. "We that dwell in the Light hold Music as sacred," Michael said. "It is how we communicate, how we share our thoughts and feelings. When you are happy, your happiness sings to us. We hear, join in the music, and are happy with you. It is the same with sadness. It is just a different melody. Music is in all of us. It binds us to one another. It is our highest and best form of communication." Michael fell silent. He was trying to get his point across, but as usual, the words alone were not adequate. They just didn't…sing. So, Michael began to sing. He started in a low and gentle baritone and began to build. A picture began to form in the mind. It was a panoramic view; one of vast distances over time and space. Chris felt, rather than saw, the creation of Music. "…And God opened his mouth and brought forth song. And the angels were born of the song and joined in the song…and from that song was brought forth the earth, the wind, the sky,...and man. And because God loved man, he taught men and women, through his messengers, the sacred Melodies..." Now, the Music became more quiet and introspective. Finally, it began to fade and Michael spoke again. There were tears in his eyes.

"An old woman, her mind ravaged by time, cannot even recall her own name. Yet she remembers the songs she sang as a little girl. A child, traumatized by abuse may not be able to speak; yet, he will sing with Barney, the purple lizard, or Dora the Explorer. Why do you think Music holds so much power over us? Why do you think it can make you dance, cry, or march to your death in a war you do not understand? It is because Music is a powerful force." Then the melody stopped altogether. There was a perfect, solemn, quiet. "Why," Michael asked, "did the great Musicians of the past always, always dedicate and give credit to God and Heaven for their great works; their inspiration?"

Silence followed, as if every great and small tunesmith from the street musician to the concert maestro had to ponder a profound mystery. The answer came back quietly, but with the force of revelation, the silence broken by the voice of Michael. "...It is because Music is a gift from God. No less."

Then, Michael smiled, his mood less somber. "And you are a drummer! The heartbeat of the Sacred Music. Chris, Musicians in general, and drummers in particular, are held in high regard in the Light. They are close to God! It used to be so in this world! I know that money is important. I know you want to help your father, but you must look at the larger picture."

There was silence while Chris let it sink in. "I don't know," he said. "It's good to know I am appreciated...but why are you telling me this? It seems like a lot of hype over one drummer."

"It only takes the influence of one soul, or the lack of it, to make a difference," said Michael. He could see that Chris was not quite convinced. He continued. "...And, you are a special case."

Chris looked up. "Huh?" He pointed to himself. "Me?"

"We lost the Music once," began Michael. "Actually, it was stolen, and we had to fight to get it back." Michael saw that he had piqued some interest. He continued..."It was a music maker, like you, that helped us...one about your age."

"Really?," Chris asked. "You're kidding, right?" This sounded like it could be a good story.

"Yes, really," replied Michael. "You know the story."

"What story?," asked Chris.

Michael saw that this was how he would convince Chris of his worth. "The story of the Nativity," said Michael, "in song."

Chris looked puzzled.

"You know,...*Silent Night*, *O Holy Night*,...He began to sing. "Oh come, oh come Emmanuel..."

"Oh!" said Chris. "Well, yeah, I've heard those songs." It had begun to dawn on Chris that this man? Crazy person? whatever, was...he didn't know. *Is it true?* "So, what are you?"

Michael didn't answer. Could this boy make the leap between logic and faith...to believe...in that which is unseen? "There was a boy," he replied finally. "...who brought the Music back to us and changed the world in one night. Yes, I was there."

"Right," was all Chris could say.

Michael came closer. "Would you like to hear the story? The real and true story of how the music was brought back to us?"

"Okay," said Chris.

"Do you think it might convince you to stay with the music?"

“Couldn’t hurt,” replied Chris, outwardly nonchalant but inwardly curious. He still wasn’t buying it, but he would play along.

“Good,” said Michael. “Lay back and close your eyes. I’ll dream it to you.”

“Dream it to me?,” asked Chris.

“Yes,” said Michael. “Trust me, the effects are much better.” His eyes widened on the word MUCH. Chris lay down and closed his eyes. Michael sat down in the chair next to the bed. He was excited. Oh, how he loved a good story. He began: “Many, many generations of man ago, in a place you really wouldn’t want to be, a plan was laid…”

"Where words fail, music speaks."

—HANS CHRISTIAN ANDERSON

CHAPTER 2:

A BAD PLACE TO BE

Suddenly, Chris and Michael were somewhere and somewhen else. They stood in what looked like a throne room, on either side of a large chair, which sat atop a dais, looking down on what appeared to be thousands of prostrate bodies. Chris felt that the room, the very walls, were waiting for something, a command perhaps, or instructions. He couldn't feel heat, but the air seemed to ripple like it was very hot, as if coming from the back of a jet engine. The figure on the throne, hooded and cloaked in black, looked deep in thought. Again, there was that feeling of anticipation; the very air around them seemed to be waiting for something to happen. Chris leaned back behind the chair to catch Michael's eye. He wanted to ask what was going on. Even though it was obviously a dream, it felt very real. He had Michael's attention and saw Michael put his finger to his lips to signify quiet.

Chris mouthed the words, *Where are we?*

Michael mouthed back, *You'll see.* He then put a finger to his lips again, more earnestly this time.

Presently the figure in the chair, which up to now had been completely still, stirred...To his surprise and horror, Chris realized that what he thought was the back of a large ornate throne was actually a quite large pair of folded, black wings. The figure moved in a kind of casual, stretching gesture. When he did, one of the wings shot out from the chair so fast the rush of air knocked Chris off balance and he would have fallen backward if Michael had not caught him. Chris took a good look at that wing before it was retracted back to the shoulder in the blink of an eye. Obviously, the laws of physics did not apply here. Something that big could not possibly move that fast.

Chris stifled a gasp as Michael continued to hold him. The wing looked like it belonged to a gigantic raven, so black and shiny it was tinged with blue. It was as large as a sail—six feet wide at the base and twice as long. The primary feathers were larger than a man's arm. A stench of rotting flesh emanated from the wing, and Chris would have thrown up if he hadn't been so scared. He wanted out of there now, dream or nightmare he didn't care, but now he saw what had caused the figure to stir. Someone was coming. The bodies, still prostrate, were turning their heads and parting as another figure, also hooded and cloaked, walked through them toward the throne. This one obviously commanded respect, judging from the way the prostrate throng parted and avoided his gaze. He approached the first step just before the dais of the throne, bowed his head down low, and bent down on one knee.

"Lord," was all he said. His voice was between a hiss and a whisper and even though he was several feet away, Chris had no problem hearing every word said. His voice carried in this place. All voices carried. It was as if there could be no secrets from the one on the throne. All voices and all thoughts were captured and revealed to him. It made Chris uneasy. He was afraid to whisper, afraid even to think. He would be captured.

"Speak," said the throned figure in a dark, reverberating bass tone, which Chris could both hear and feel with his ears and his mind. Chris was surprised that the voice was actually not unpleasant. This frightened him, and then he realized why. It would be hard to resist a voice like that. He felt an involuntary chill, like a warning. All the figure had said was one word, and Chris felt compelled to tell his deepest, darkest secrets. He felt that if he stayed any longer, he might want to bow down and worship. He began to panic.

"The Child," said the figure, the one on bended knee. Chris surmised that he must be some kind of high-ranking servant returning from an errand.

"Yes," said the sinister bass voice. "Speak to me of the Child."

"He will be born soon," said the hiss-whisper. "The star grows brighter. It is the great confluence; the fulfillment of the prophecy."

Silence. Chris knew the one on the throne only waited. The servant continued, "Herod has sent three old fools, wise men they are called," his contempt for them obvious. "They are to find the child and send word. When they find him, he will send assassins to kill the Child."

"Mmmm," said the throned one, nodding his head, "…this Herod… he is easily manipulated."

"Yes," came the reply. "I merely convinced him that the Child was a threat to his power. He is a fool and does our bidding willingly and unwittingly, my lord."

"Good," came the dark, bass reply. Then came the loud, boisterous, insane laugh. Chris held his ears, as the sound seemed to split his eardrums and make them bleed through his fingers. He screamed inside. The throned one spoke, "This world is mine! He shall not have it! Already, the hate congeals like blood on the battlefield. The Child will not be born!" At this last outburst, a wail rose up from the prostrate bodies before him and the air seemed to ripple even more.

After the wailing calmed, the dark voice spoke again: "Is there word of the talisman?"

The reply was hesitant. "Yes, lord. My spies tell me there is a rumor of a shepherd boy. It is said he tames the animals with his voice. He sings to them."

"And?" came the dark reply.

There was more hesitation this time. "He has not been found, lord."

The dark one then leaned forward and motioned for his servant to come closer. Although he spoke softly, Chris heard every word. He also heard a name. "Belial," he whispered, "Find him. Tend to it personally. Go."

There was no need to ask what would happen if this boy was not found.

The servant gone, the room and images faded and Chris and Michael were once again alone. Chris took a deep breath. He hadn't realized he'd been holding it. "Jesus," he said.

"Jesus has nothing to do with it," Michael replied, "...and don't use His name like that."

Michael waited again for questions. "Told you the effects were good," he said.

Chris looked at Michael. "Was that...?"

"Yes," Michael answered matter of factly. "He is the adversary."

"But what was he doing? What was he talking about?," Chris asked. "What child does he want not to be born?"

"Well," Michael said, "...think about it. Think about it within a biblical context."

"Huh?," was all Chris could say.

"The Bible!" said Michael. "You know, big black book."

Chris looked at Michael as if he'd watched TV all night instead of studying and then been hit with a pop quiz. "The Bible!!," reiterated

Michael. "There was mention of Herod, the king, a shining star, the birth of a Child, come on! This is easy!"

"Oh, Christmas!" yelled Chris.

"Yes!" Michael then mumbled something about the present state of education under his breath.

"So, this…"Chris was still trying to get his head around just who this was on the dark throne, "…he wanted to kill the Christ child!"

"Thank you!," said Michael.

"But why?" asked Chris.

"Why?" repeated Michael. "I don't know. Why does one child stray and the other does not, even though they are both loved equally? We were given wondrous things, the gift of flight, foresight, and Music."

"Music?" asked Chris.

"Yes," replied Michael. "It was our greatest and most powerful gift." Michael closed his eyes and was still. He seemed to be somewhere else. Then he spoke again. "I do not know why he left us." Then he opened his eyes and turned to Chris., "…but we have been fighting ever since."

"So," Michael continued, "…if you are a powerful member of the fallen, the dark adversary, recently arrived from the holy light, the world is your oyster! You are the man! The last thing you want is competition, especially if He is going to be the Savior of the world. Best to prevent him from being born, or do away with him while he is young and helpless."

"I still don't understand why," said Chris.

"Free will," said Michael. "We all have it. The difference is he chose to impose his will on others. He was, after all, the first created. He was gifted with great power to influence many things. And so, there was war. He was defeated and cast out, along with his followers. And on that day the great chasm was created, his separation from The Light, and since then he and his have been the vexation of Humankind."

Chris was silent while he pondered the implications. He had never thought of that particular Bible story as the break-up of a family. "What about the Music?" asked Chris. "You keep mentioning it like it is some kind of weapon."

Michael looked at Chris. "You see things in such simplistic terms. Everything is black or white. You see Music as harmless entertainment, an accompaniment to a movie or themes to your favorite Netflix show. It is much more than that. Music is a force, a force of nature, no less powerful than a tornado, a hurricane, or any other act of God. Handel, Bach, Beethoven, they understood. Music has power and anything that has power can be a weapon."

Chris was intrigued by this concept. He had not thought of music as a force of nature. It made sense, though. Now he understood why he felt the way he did when he played. He felt power!

"…And much of the power in music comes from the drums, the heartbeat of the music," continued Michael. "It is the focus, the drive of the music. Ever since the first man picked up a stick and struck a hollow log, the drum has been used to communicate, to inspire, and to connect the sacred pathways." Michael turned to Chris. "Do you see now, how special you are?"

"I think I'm beginning to get it. Music is power!"

"Excellent!" said Michael. "And that is why he took it from us."

"I don't understand," said Chris. "How could he do that?"

"He was the strongest of us all, second only to the Almighty himself," said Michael. "He laid his plans well, and when the time was right, he took the Music from us. It doesn't matter how. I suppose he thought to use it against us in the last battle. He clearly did not expect to be defeated. He was very prideful, and that was his downfall. Anyway, somehow, he took the music from us and placed it in a container, for lack of a better word. It was a plain-looking shepherd staff, but a talisman of immense power. He was not able to use it against us in the last battle. I struggled with him, but he was strong. I drew the flaming sword and struck the talisman from his hand. It fell to earth, and the battle continued another hundred years before he was finally defeated. We did not know what he had done until we tried to join in song after our victory. We raised our voices to the Light and behold…nothing happened. We couldn't even sing of our great sorrow, for that too required knowledge of the Sacred Melodies. We searched for years, but could not find the staff. The time passed."

"Meanwhile," continued Michael, "…humankind grew and developed. Still we searched, as did he, but the staff could not be found. Finally, a prophecy was given to us that a Savior would be born under a new star and that on that night the music would be returned."

"Christmas!" shouted Chris.

"Bingo," said Michael. "And the world turned." Chris was hooked. He had even more questions now. Michael smiled; he'd always been a good storyteller.

"So," asked Chris, "…if God created Him, and he was causing all this trouble, why doesn't he take him out?"

"Excuse me?" asked Michael.

"You know," said Chris. "Why doesn't He, you know, un-create him?"

"Chris," Michael said in an exasperated tone, "this is not a video game. Everything, every being has a purpose. Some we see as evil, some not. Do they deserve to perish? Perhaps, but that is not our purpose. We do not judge. We do not destroy a thing simply because it seems evil to us. That is not our way." Michael then looked up. "It is not His way. We do not know why evil exists. Nor do we know its purpose. We simply know to fight it. That is our purpose. We hope for redemption, but we keep our shields and swords at the ready."

Christopher realized that there would be no more discussion of divine destruction, but he wasn't finished yet. He would push the envelope a little more. "Alright," he said. "So, no uncreating this…bad guy. Maybe he has some purpose we don't know about, but you did defeat him the first time with some kind of a…"

"…flaming sword," said Michael.

"Right," said Chris, "…so why don't you just use the sword to beat him again?"

"Because," Michael said "…the same prophecy that told of the coming of the Christ Child and the return of the music also foretold another event…" Michael took a deep breath. "When next the flaming sword is drawn, then will be the earth's last dawn."

The realization shone on Chris's face. "Do you mean…"

"…the end of days," said Michael. "The sword has a destiny to fulfill. If I draw the sword, it will do just that."

"Damn," said Chris.

"'Scuse me?," said Michael.

"Sorry," said Chris.

Michael nodded and locked eyes with Chris. "I am Michael, the sword of The Light; yet, I do not know His purpose for all things. I do what is given to me to do and I try to sway others of free will to do what is right and true, but I am not all powerful…and neither is my dark brother."

"So, okay," said Chris, "…Jesus was born and the music was returned, so the prophecy came true."

"Correct," said Michael.

"How?" repeated Chris." To quote an old Beatle's song…with a little help from my friends…' actually a lot of help," said Michael.

"Well," said Chris, "…your friends must've been regular action heroes!"

"No," answered Michael. "…more like actual heroes; a boy and a girl, about your age. There was nothing action-hero-like about them. They had no Light power and no flaming sword. They did have, however, great strength of character. They knew what was right and they knew what had to be done. Together, they saved the child, returned the Sacred Music, and fulfilled the prophecy."

Chris was still, in fact dreaming, and the entire conversation with Michael had taken place within that dream. But now the dream was changing from nowhere in particular to somewhere more definite. "How did they do it?" He felt solid ground under his feet now, and heard something, something like…sheep?

"You're about to find out," came Michael's answer.

"There is music in all things, if men had ears;

the earth is but the music of the spheres."

—LORD BYRON

CHAPTER 3:

STUPID SHEEP

It was night, somewhere in the semi-arid desert. Chris could definitely hear the bleating of sheep. Michael was standing beside him.

"Where are we?," asked Chris.

Michael put a finger to his lips. "Shhhh," he said. "Watch and listen…for this is your story."

"My story?" Chris asked. "What do you mean my story?"

Silence. Michael was gone.

A boy about Chris's age and build, but darker of complexion, came over a small rise. He was singing. He had a staff with strange markings on it, a jingling bell, and several feathers attached to strip of leather. He had a high, soft, tenor voice, which flowed effortlessly from him and into the cool, desert night. As Chris looked on, he was amazed. He saw by the moonlight that the sheep followed the boy in pairs. They went two by two one right after the other, but that was not the strangest thing. Running up and down beside the sheep were several large wolves. They appeared to be guarding the sheep! When a lamb strayed from the line, a large lobo with equally large teeth gently nudged the baby back in step. There was no howling or barking or nipping at the heels, just an ever-so-gentle nudge back to Mother. In the distance was a welcoming campfire. When all of the sheep were settled around the fire, the wolves broke off their guardianship and loped off into the night.

"Thank you, my friends! Tomorrow night, then, and good hunting!" the shepherd called. They howled back in return and were gone. The boy and sheep settled for the night, the stars keeping watch. In the morning, the shepherd boy was awakened by a strange sound.

"Heeeyyyyou! Get o-ver here! Now!!! No, No, No! Here, Here, here!…Not thererrrrrrrrrr! Here! Over here! Now! Plleeeeeeeeeeeze?… Oh!…Stupid sheep!" Definitely a female voice, coming from the east and not very far away. The shepherd boy kept walking toward the sound. Finally, he stepped to the top of a small hill, which overlooked a dry creek bed, and there she was—what looked like a slender shepherd girl, berating a small flock of sheep milling around aimlessly, seemingly shepherd-less. "Stupid sheep! Stupid, stupid, stupid! Dumb animals!"

While this harangue continued, the boy decided to go down for a closer look. He had quietly come up behind her and was trying to figure out how to announce himself when she suddenly turned around and came face to face with him.

"Aaaah!" she yelled, as she clutched her heart in surprise. "Jeez!" she said, "Don't do that! You scared me to death!" She began to calm down a little, placed her hands on her hips, and gave the boy a disapproving look. "You shouldn't sneak up on people like that. It's not nice."

There was a moment of unrehearsed silence. "What?!" she said, her exasperation showing. "Is there something between my teeth?" She slid a fingernail between her teeth as unobtrusively as possible to check for leftovers. The shepherd boy then realized he was staring, but he couldn't help it. This girl…this girl was…well suffice to say he was surprised to see a girl like this in the wilderness, standing in the middle of a flock of sheep. She had a strong, confident, no-nonsense outer attitude wrapped

about a soft, sensitive inner self that the boy instinctively kne
very few special individuals had been privileged to experience. An
seeing the reason he was staring at her, she smiled ever so slightly
almost heard the sound of a page turning, a new chapter beginning. H
life would never be the same.

Her defiant posture softened a bit. "You don't get many girls around here, do you?" she said.

"Uhm…" he stammered.

"I am Mira," she said, her smile broadening.

His heart was thumping, palms were sweaty, and knees were weak. *Say something!* came the panicked, high-pitched plea to himself. She had not used the first voice he had heard, the one scolding the unruly sheep. This was the coo of a dove, the brushing of an angel's wing against the cheek. Woefully unprepared, he was not ready for this. No, he was not ready for…

"Hello. Did you hear me?"

And he was slammed back to here and now. "Huh? What?" was all his befuddled brain could muster.

"I said my name is Mira. I am daughter to Malakai and sister to Rahsheed. I live…"

Finally, a reference point. "I know where you live," interrupted the shepherd boy. "I know Rahsheed. He never mentioned he had a sister"

"I'm sure he had his reasons," she said with an edge to her voice she was unable to hide. "He never thought of anyone but himself," she said more to herself than the shepherd boy. "He has run away with a caravan. He never wanted to be a shepherd. My father has no more sons, so I must take care of the sheep, and here I am." She looked down at her feet, then up to the shepherd boy. "I am not a very good shepherd," she said dejectedly.

: shepherd boy saw his opportunity and took it. "If you would can…"

"I do not need you or any male to see to my father's sheep for me," ..e said defiantly. Then she adopted a more humble posture. "…but if you could…help…I would be grateful."

""Yes," the boy said. "I would be most happy to show you how to… help you take care of your father's sheep. You are the daughter of Malkai, my father's friend. It is reason enough. I am Christopher, son of Jethro." And somewhere, a witness named Chris became more aware of his place in the world.

"It's easy, really. You just sing." Christopher began to sing in his lilting tenor voice. The sheep had begun to wander, but now they stopped and seemed to be listening. They began to walk toward the voice. Mira was speechless. Her eyes widened and her jaw dropped open. Soon, all the sheep were gathered round in a circle, looking up at the two as if awaiting instructions.

"You get them to do this by singing?" she asked, sarcastically.

"Of course," he said. "…to the sheep…" she repeated. "You sing to the sheep, and that's how you…"

"take care of them," Christopher finished.

"Christopher," she said with a voice of authority, "I have been around sheep and shepherds all my life, and I know of no one but you who sings to sheep…" She stopped in mid-sentence… "unless…"

Her eyes widened. "…Wait, I have heard of you, but I thought it was just a story!" A thoughtful look came to her face. "Do you carry a drum?"

In response, Christopher untied something that had been dangling from his staff. It appeared to be a thin, flexible piece of wood with some kind of animal skin tied to it. He threaded the wood through a series of ringlets around the perimeter of the skin, which was round in shape.

Then he tied the ends of the stick together. When he was finished, he had a perfectly round hand-drum which, when struck with his hand, gave out a deep, resonant Thruuuummmm sound.

"Yes," Christopher said proudly. "…I carry a drum ." He closed his eyes and, putting himself in a trance-like state, began to play. He started with a simple heartbeat rhythm: thuuuummmm ta thuuuuuummm ta thuuuuummm tathuuuuummm…Along with this, he alternately spoke or hummed a tune. It was not a popular or catchy tune Mira was accustomed to, pleasant ditties to while the time away. This was an ancient melody, perhaps hundreds of years old. The desert was still and the sheep quiet. All listened in anticipation.

Thuuuuummm ta Thuuuuuuummmm ta…The land has a rhythm… Thuuuummm…age to age…ta thuuuuummm…season to season… day…thuuummmm ta…night…thuuuuummm." He began to sway with the rhythm.

"Always and never…" The drum began to spin, almost as if it lived, given life by its own heartbeat. Christopher was no longer Christopher. He had been transformed into something greater. He was one with the sacred heartbeat, the rhythm master. The rhythm remained the same, but now the timbre of the drum changed by being struck with different parts of the hand. tahUUUuuummm tah tahUUUuuummm tah tahUUUuuummmtah…Mira, eyes closed, began to sway. The whole desert seemed to be moving. The Joshua tree, the cactus, the desert animals, even the stars overhead circled around the source, the rhythm master.

Mira saw images in her mind; there stood Christopher. He faced something menacing, although she could not see who or what it was. The drum was a shield, the shepherd staff a rod with an unnatural glow. Behind Christopher stood a figure of a man, bathed in white light. He held something. Christopher's voice broke in, "Darkness and light… good…evil…"

TahUUUuuummm tah Thuummm ta Thumm. The playing was faster now, like the heartbeat of someone running for their life, quick and frantic. Ta thum ta thum ta…then a scream. "He is coming!"

The spell broken, Mira quickly opened her eyes to find Christopher lying on his back, his eyes open but unseeing, clutching his staff and drum close to him, breathing fast, feverish. She took his face in her hands and called his name softly. "Christopher ." Suddenly, he was aware of someone next to him. "No! You shall not have it!" He shouted desperately. He struggled to get away, but she held onto him.

"Christopher! Hey! It's me!" she shouted. Finally, he was fully awake.

He looked into her eyes. "It is the dream again," he said.

After a few minutes, Christopher began to recover. He related his dream to Mira, feeling she would somehow understand. He'd had this dream since he was very young, but now there was an urgency about it, as if time was short. "A war," he said. "…War in heaven. Thousands of angels fighting, tumbling over each other in the sky…and then falling… everywhere. There are great, dark, billowing thunderclouds, casting out tornados of fire and shards of lightning."

"Then the clouds separate, and I realize that they are not thunderclouds at all, but two angels, one of bright light, the other a dark reddish like spilt blood."

Christopher's eyes were filled with tears of wonder and fear. "… fighting…struggling…lighting up the air with their power, their fury. They are the last two, the leaders, Light and Dark…enemies…adversaries…" He turned to face her. "…but also brothers. There is a great explosion of light and thunder, and the clouds begin to dissipate. As the clouds disperse, from the midst of them comes a bright light, falling to earth like a shooting star. I mark the path and run to where I think it will strike. Finally, I arrive at the place. There is smoke rising from the ground with the scent of burning incense all around. I run to the source of the smoke and do you know what I find?"

Mira shook her head. Christopher thrust out his shepherd staff to her. "This," he said. "Hold it."

She took the staff from his hand gingerly. "It's warm," she said. "It always is, even on the coldest nights," he said. Then he took the staff from her hand and cast it into the fire.

"What are you doing?" she asked. She tried to intervene, but he held her fast.

"Watch," he said.

She watched and, as she did, the reality washed over her. She turned to him. "It does not burn," she said.

"No," he said. He took the staff from the fire. It had not even been lightly scorched, the surface unmarked. "This staff has been passed from father to son in my family for generations. It has never shown signs of decay."

"It is said that holy things are incorruptible," said Mira.

"Yes," said Christopher. "That is true."

They both sat, deep in thought. Finally, Mira looked up and said what they both were thinking: "I think you'd better keep both eyes on that staff."

"Yes," said Christopher.

"It's late," she said. "Would you watch my flock? I must go home and discuss these things with my father. He is wise. Perhaps he will know what to do."

He was happy that she trusted him with her sheep. It was her way of paying him a compliment. "I will be honored to take your watch," he said with as much bravado and humility as he dared. He was glad to be doing anything for this girl. She smiled at him.

"Tomorrow then," she said.

"Uh, tomorrow," was that all he could think of to say.

As he continued to castigate himself for imagined awkwardness, as young men will do, she moved toward him. "Sleep well," she said. Then she smiled, waved, and was gone. She knew. Somehow, she knew.

Dumb smitten (dumbfounded and smitten), Christopher lay down with his hands behind his head, looked at the stars, and wondered…and wondered. It almost felt like it was meant to happen, meeting this girl. If he had known what the next day held, perhaps he would have been more inclined to get a good night's rest.

"Music is a revelation; a revelation loftier than all wisdom and all philosophy."

—LUDWIG VON BEETHOVEN

CHAPTER 4:

DREAMS, VISIONS, OLD ENEMIES, NEW FRIENDS

The following morning, Christopher was putting out the fire and getting ready to go find Mira. He had experienced a disturbing night with more disturbing dreams. They found each other at the same time. She was out of breath and clearly excited, upset, or both.

"I've got to talk to you!" they both said at the same time.

"You start," said Christopher. He gave her time to catch her breath.

"Last night," she said, still gasping, "...last night, my father saw a vision!"

"A vision?" asked Christopher.

"...An angel!"

"An angel?" Christopher repeated.

"Yes!" She was almost in tears and still breathing hard. "He was with two other shepherds, watching their flocks, and an angel appeared to them all!"

"Tell me what he said." He took her by the shoulders. "Tell me what the angel said!" She nodded her head. She had caught her breath now, but her mood was no less serious. "Tell me," he repeated once more. There were tears in her eyes. They looked at one another. He let go of her shoulders. It was if the eye of a storm was passing over them. Even the sheep appeared to be listening.

"It was mid of night. A bright light blinded them. They couldn't see, but finally their eyes adjusted. It was an angel! With wings! He said, 'Fear not, for I bring you tidings of great joy! For unto you a Savior is born. Look for him under the star in the east, in a manger…in Bethlehem!" they both finished at once. They looked at each other in surprise.

"Hey," she said, "This is my dream!"

"I know," he said, "but I also had a dream last night.

"Were there angels in yours?" she asked.

"No," said Christopher.

"Do not mock me, Christopher," she admonished.

"No, no Mira. I'm not mocking you. But I did have a dream about a child being born under a star, much like your father's vision." Then Christopher turned away. "Only mine became a nightmare."

"How?" she asked. He turned to face her. There was fear in his eyes. In his dream, he walked down a path. He recognized it as the road to Bethlehem. At the end of this path, he came upon a manger surrounded by a crowd of many people. They were of all faiths, all religions; the rich, the poor, the hopeless, and the hopeful. Even the animals gathered to see this special child. Tears came to his eyes as Christopher described the child. "His face…his face was filled with light. And the light filled everyone and everything around with hope. All people joined together in one moment."

Then Christopher described how a shadow passed before him. The people turned and there was terror in their eyes. The baby began to cry "…and the crying got louder and louder!" There was panic in his voice now. He clamped his hands over his ears to stop it. He began to cry. And Mira held him while he cried and rocked him because he was hers and she was his and it was as it should be. And she knew this to be true for she had also dreamed of a premonition; one that she would keep within her own heart.

After a while, Christopher calmed down. When he looked up, the panic in his eyes had been replaced by a resolve made of steel instead. "We have to save him, Mira."

With resolve equal to his, she simply nodded her head and replied, "We will leave tonight ." Her dream, kept safe in her heart, would have to wait…"and may God be with us," she added.

"He will be there," said Christopher. And he knew not the portent of those spoken words.

Again, the scene began to shift. Chris had almost forgotten that he was dreaming, watching a documentary in his mind that had transpired centuries before. Again, it was Chris and Michael behind the throne of the black-winged creature: "…Escaped?! You let him…escape?!!" Chris held his ears. The horizontal bodies and the wayward servant did as well.

"They must have been warned, lord!" Belial screamed in anguish, anticipating his punishment. "It must have been Michael!"

"Do not say that name!" The dark angel half hissed, half screamed. Belial was obviously trying to divert attention away from himself.

"Forgive me, lord, but you know he has ever been jealous of you!!"

"Silence!" said the dark-winged giant. And there was. None dared breathe. Even the strange ripple in the air diminished. Lucifer calmed himself.

"Michael…," and he sighed a strange sigh of regret and of loss. "Michael is too pure to know jealousy." He turned back to the servant. "So, the child has escaped. Have you found the staff?"

"Yes, lord," he replied, relieved that he had some news that would please his dark master. "The shepherd boy possesses it. He is on his way to the birthplace of the child. Shall I take it from him?"

"No, fool!" said his master. "It cannot be taken from him. It must be given up freely. Does he know its secrets?" The servant remained silent, nervous that there was something he didn't know. (This was a master you simply did not ask questions, like, "Pardon?" or "'scuse me? I didn't get your meaning.") The master closed his eyes and seemed to be somewhere else. Then he continued, "I sense that the power of the staff still sleeps. That is well. Michael will not draw the sword, but if he obtains the talisman, he could stop me ."

Then he turned once more to his underling. "You will get the staff. Find a way to make him give it to you freely."

"Yes, lord," he said, relieved that he could still be of service, "…and what of the child?"

"I will deal with the child after he is born. He will still be weak." Once more, he directed his gaze upon the servant. "Now go," he said. "And do not fail me again. There are still many ways to suffer." The threat was not lost. The servant turned and was gone.

The next day found Christopher and Mira on the road to Bethlehem. They did not know what they would find. They only knew to be ready for…"Lucifer? Pllleeease, I don't think so," said Mira.

"Can you think of any other explanation?" asked Christopher.

"Yes," she said. "My father…" She said, dramatically with hand on chest, "had a vision! You had a bad dream ."

Christopher was about to beg to differ when they came across a very strange sight.

"Hello, my friends! Hello! Hirsute Harry at your service!" What they now viewed was one of the most bizarre scenes ever seen before or since. Across their path stood a giant tent with a portly person in front of it, motioning them inside. Had it been there a moment before?

He wore a black robe with a red sash and had a large turban upon his head. His name fit him well, for he was very hairy, even on his knuckles, and he had one single, large, bushy eyebrow across his forehead. His smile was very white and toothy, which lent a bit of a carnivorous look to his already unsavory appearance. The two travelers instinctively did not trust him. They looked at one another and each knew that they would keep this stranger at arm's length.

"Hiyah, hiyah, hiyah! Get your shepherd staffs right heahh! Every size! Every color! Even got 'His 'n Hers!' One for the gentleman and one for the lady! Or I'll give you gold on a trade! Hiyah! Hiyah! Hiyah!"

They stopped at the entrance to the tent and looked in.

"Please, please, my friends! Come in! Come in! See what I have to offer! A treasure. A treasure, I promise you!" Harry was an interesting character. As Chris (still dreaming) looked on, he realized that Harry reminded him of a cross between a used car salesman and a doorman at a five-star hotel. They walked in. Everywhere they looked were shepherd staffs in every size, shape, and color one could imagine. Short, tall, thick, and thin, they were everywhere, amazing and unreal, especially since shepherds don't ever buy a staff. It is either handed down to them or they make their own. Christopher and Mira looked around, then at one another, then at this very strange person staring at them, grinning from ear to ear, his predatory shark teeth unnaturally white.

"You sell shepherd staffs?" asked Christopher. The trickster nodded; his expression unchanged.

"But, no one sells shepherd staffs," Christopher remarked as nonchalantly as he could.

"Precisely!" he said. "I'm getting in on the ground floor." He secretly nudged Christopher in the ribs and then in a low voice whispered, "I'll make a killing!"

The glee in his eyes when he said *killing* was not lost on Christopher. He then straightened and, putting on a business-like demeanor, pulled out a pencil and parchment and asked, "How many do I put you down for?"

"None," said Christopher flatly. "I'm happy with the one I've got."

Harry was not discouraged. "Oh, what do you want with that ol' thing! HAH! Hiyah, such a deal I have for you!" He tried to put an arm around Christopher's shoulder, but Christopher would have none of that. Harry just kept talking. An endless tirade of every huckster sales pitch known to man…"Ya seem like a good kid, but I won't hold it against ya! HAAAHHHH, HA HAHAAAaaa, OHHhhh, I am killing myself! Did you get it, kid? It's a joke…"

Christopher and Mira looked on in disbelief. They were, after all, in the middle of nowhere. The odds of this person being here at this time were…

"When does he breathe?" asked Mira.

"I don't know," answered Christopher. "Maybe he gets a quick breath in between those big teeth when he's laughing."

"Kid! It's funny! Don't you…"

"I get it. I get it," said Christopher.

Harry was getting obnoxious. He pointed to Christopher's staff. "I'll take that ol' stick of yours and give you a brand-new staff plus two gold pieces!"

Christopher looked at Mira, rolled his eyes, and turned to the man. "I really don't…"

"…but wait! There's more!" Harry interrupted.

Christopher abruptly ended Harry's speech by holding up his hand. "I said 'No, thanks.'" Christopher thought he had turned away, but suddenly Harry was in front of him. Christopher was thinking to himself how Harry moved remarkably fast for a large person when a large sack of gold appeared in Harry's large, meaty hand from out of nowhere. This was the second time something had appeared from out of nowhere.

"Alright, sonny," Harry said, feigning regret. "You drive a hard bargain. The gold is yours. Just give me the staff and I'll be on my way." Now, things were getting strange. What Christopher was being offered was many times what a supposedly worthless piece of wood should be valued. Christopher looked Harry squarely in the eye and calm came over him. He had never been so sure of anything in his life. First, Harry was not human, and second, no way was he letting go of his staff.

"No," he said with as much finality and fearlessness as he could muster. He was afraid. Very afraid. Something in the eyes of Harry was not ... just as quickly as the gold appeared, it suddenly disappeared and in its place was a very ugly, very sharp dagger. This was not a knife used for protection. This was a killing tool, a bloodletting blade; an evil thing possessed by an evil being.

"Wrong answer, boy," said the being. Christopher had never been faced with a situation like this. He was frozen. Mira, on the other hand, had lived with brothers. She had never encountered a situation quite like this, but she had been on the wrong end of jokes and surprises many times, thanks to her loving siblings. This had enabled her to develop a keen sense of the here it comes just before it came. She had a staff too and Harry, having discounted her as a mere female, had forgotten all about her; a mistake that would be made many times by many unwitting males through the centuries. Mira's staff, unexpected and well aimed, came down hard upon the wrist of the knife-hand with a loud crack.

That was a very satisfying sound to Mira, along with the accompanying cry of pain and anger.

In the blink of an eye, the other hand came up to rip the precious staff from the hands of Christopher. He held onto the staff as if his life depended on it, which it did. He knew that once this creature with the clamp-like grip had the staff, all pretense of bargains would be at an end. He was losing. Soon now, very soon…

"You can't take it."

"Huh?" said all three as they turned. What they saw was a tall man (more than six feet), with a square jaw, and ice blue eyes, who looked very much like and in fact was Michael.

"It has to be given over freely," said Michael. "But, surely you know that." He was looking very intently at Harry. "The one who created it wished it so, did he not? So that it could not be stolen?"

Harry, still gripping the staff, only had time to say one thing: "You!" Then, he screamed and gripped his hand, which had somehow been burned by holding the staff.

"Told you," said Michael.

"You" Harry said a second time.

"Yes, it's me," said Michael. "It has been a long time…Harry, is it?"

Harry took a step toward Michael, bellowing in rage as Christopher and Mira looked on in shock and befuddlement. "You cast me out!" said Harry in anger, and perhaps a little pain. "You can come back." Michael replied.

Harry looked up at Michael, a mixture of fear and hope in his eyes. Michael took a step forward, arms open, palms up. "All you have to do is…"

"I know what I have to do," said Harry. "I will not beg on my knees for forgiveness."

"Then just say you're sorry," said Michael. Harry did not reply, but looked away.

"I see," said Michael, "better to rule in hell…"

Harry's face twisted in rage. He took a step toward Michael.

"You cannot win," said Michael. Harry stopped and lowered the knife. "My master says otherwise," he said.

"…and he is strong."

"Then go to your master," Michael said calmly, "and take your circus with you."

Harry and the tent of merchandise began to fade. "You will have to draw your sword, Michael! This is not over!" screamed Harry, his voice filled with anger and pain and resentment, for he was outcast…and then he was gone. Mira and Christopher looked at each other, then at this stranger standing next to them.

"How do you know that man?" she asked.

"A long time ago," Michael mused, "you might say we had a falling out."

Christopher was still in shock. "He was going to kill me for my staff."

"No, I don't think so," Michael stated nonchalantly. "You saw what happened to his hand. It cannot be taken. It must be given up freely."

"How do you know that?" asked Mira, "and…and who are you anyway?"

Michael explained that he travelled a lot and had heard stories about a talisman of power. He was telling the truth, of course, just not all of it. "My name is Michael, and I am on my way to Bethlehem, as it appears you are also." Michael knew that they were suspicious of him and hoped that by giving them his name and business, they would be less so.

Christopher spoke first. "I am Christopher. This is Mira. We are bound for Bethlehem also." Both of them had noticed a rather large sword strapped to the back of this intimidating man, which would make anyone traveling on the same road nervous. Too, this large sword-bearing stranger happening along in the nick of time, as it were, was just a tad coincidental.

"Why are you going to Bethlehem?" asked Mira. Michael looked at her. It was a blunt, even rude question to ask a stranger who quite possibly had just saved her life. Still, they needed to be suspicious of all strangers from now on. He knew who they were up against.

"An event is going to take place in Bethlehem," he said with a smile. "An event long awaited. I am going to go see it."

Mira was not yet satisfied. "Does this event have anything to with the birth of a child?"

"Mira!" admonished Christopher. "He doesn't need to know…"

"Too late, Christopher," she said. "He knows, and I do not think it mere chance that he happened along when he did," she added as she attempted to burn a hole in Michael with her eyes. She turned back to Christopher, the look in her eyes sincere, her tone more gentle. "The time for secrecy is over, Christopher. We need to know if he is friend or foe…"

Then, she turned back to Michael, looking at him intently, trying to see through him, wanting to know what was in his heart. "And we need to know now." Michael was not ready to reveal all to this desert-hardened girl who was obviously trying to protect this naive and entirely too trusting youth. Still, they needed to know in whom they could place their trust. That would be Michael.

"If I wanted to hurt you, I could have done so and not wasted time talking about it, or I could have let Harry do the job for me."

"Are you a mercenary?" asked Mira.

"No," said Michael. "You may say that I am a soldier in the service of a great king." He put up his hand to forestall any more questions "…

and I mean you no harm." That seemed to satisfy them. He continued, "We are all going to Bethlehem. You both could use some protection and I could use some company. I propose we travel together."

Christopher and Mira looked at each other. Michael had a point. Under the circumstances, it seemed the best thing to do.

"Alright," said Christopher. "We will go to Bethlehem together."

"Excellent!" said Michael. And so, the three continued on down the road, but Mira resolved to keep a close eye on the man with the sword.

"Music is love in search of a word."

—SIDNEY LANIER

CHAPTER 5:

THE ROAD TO BETHLEHEM

There were no further attempts on Christopher's life or his staff, and the three concentrated on getting to Bethlehem. Apparently, Michael and his sword were sufficiently intimidating. Two nights later, they sat around a warm and friendly campfire. Christopher and Mira had overcome heir initial shyness. They were both curious about Michael. They had not travelled much, and knew little of the wide world. Michael, on the other hand, had travelled and was a warrior as well. They were convinced he had some stories to tell.

"So, have you been in many battles?" asked Mira.

"Some," replied Michael. Then there was silence with only the occasional pop from the fire. Clearly, Michael was not going to give any information unless it was dragged out of him.

"Uhmm...ever lost any?" Christopher pursued gently.

"None," said Michael as he looked into the fire. "...came close once."

Now they were intrigued. "Really? Tell us about it!" said Mira. She had a reason to keep the conversation going. Tomorrow they would be in Bethlehem, and she really didn't want to think about what might happen. "Come on, tell us! He must've been a great warrior to have almost beaten you."

Michael, still gazing into the fire, nodded his head. "Yes, he was a great warrior; strong and fearless."

Then he turned to Mira. "Can we talk about something else?" He looked at Christopher. "Where did you get this staff? It's very unusual, isn't it? May I?" Michael held out his hand to receive the staff. Christopher nodded. He couldn't believe he was handing it over so easily, but, for some reason, he felt he could trust this man, if that was all he was.

"Do you recognize the runes along the side?" Christopher asked as he pointed to them.

"Oh yes," Michael said, as he ran his fingers across the staff. "This is an ancient language. The speech of the sons of the most High. It is called 'Enochian..' These are words of power." He looked up at Christopher. "… and warning."

Christopher and Mira were both taken aback. "What? What warning?'" asked Mira. "Is it safe?"

"Of course," Michael said as he tossed the staff back to Christopher nonchalantly.

Perhaps it was a trick of the firelight, but Christopher would have sworn that the staff was giving off a faint glow before Michael tossed it back, and he thought he heard a sound as well, like a low, resonant hum. There was nothing now. He turned to Mira. "Did you hear…?"

There was a long pause, as he looked at Mira, then to Michael, then Mira again.

"Did I hear what?" she asked.

"Never mind." Christopher decided to change the subject. "Tell us more about your victories, Michael." They had always heard that fighters loved to boast of their victories.

As if reading their mind, Michael spoke to that thought. "True warriors do not boast. They wish only to forget."

"Who was he, Michael?" asked Christopher.

Michael continued to stare into the fire, pondering they knew not what.

Christopher sighed. Perhaps he could get Michael to trade information about his exploits in exchange for more details about the staff. "It has been in my family for generations, handed down from father to son. It does not show age and it does not burn, although it is warm to the touch, even on the coldest nights. Now, who was he, this strong and fearless warrior who almost defeated the mighty Michael?"

Michael looked at Christopher. "I said I do not wish to discuss it. The memory is…painful," said Michael.

Mira did not realize that she had crossed a line until it was too late. "But Michael…"

"I said No!" Michael had not meant to raise his voice, but it happened. The outburst was unintentional and frightening, even if only for a brief moment. Perhaps the clap of thunder was a coincidence, but the reverberation of his voice into the distance, as if echoing off of mountains would've been hard to explain. Michael looked at Christopher and Mira, immediately regretting his outburst. There was fear in their eyes…fear and awe. He had seen the look before. "Forgive me," he said. "I did not mean to frighten you." He sighed wearily. "Yes," he said "…he was a great warrior. I have never met his equal."

"And who was he?" asked Mira in an uncharacteristically shy and timid voice. She sensed his pain, and wished to give some comfort. There was a pause and another great sigh. "He was my brother," said Michael.

"You two should get some sleep," he continued in a voice that brooked no argument. "I will take the first watch. Sleep well." He climbed to a small rise, unbuckled his sword and scabbard, and sat down, the sword astride his knees, still sheathed. Christopher and Mira lay down next to each other. Neither was ready to sleep yet, although it had been a long day.

"So, what do you think of our traveling companion?" asked Mira.

Christopher wrinkled his brow, turned over on his back, and locked his hands behind his head. "It's very strange…" he mused. "Here we are, out in the middle of nowhere with this warrior, a total stranger, who possesses a large sword easily capable of removing both of our heads with one swipe…"

"And?" asked Mira after waiting several moments for him to continue. "…and I have never felt safer. I should be at least a little on my guard, but I am not."

Mira suddenly sat up on one elbow and looked down at Christopher. "Yes!" she whispered loudly. "That's exactly how I feel. It's as if I am a child back in my mother's arms. How can that be?" she asked as she lay back down.

"I do not know," answered Christopher. Then he turned to her, his head now resting on his elbow. "…but I am glad you are here, Mira."

She turned to him. "And I am glad you are with me, Christopher."

They smiled at each other in the dark, under a blanket of bright stars. "Good night, Mira."

"Sleep well, Christopher." Tomorrow, they would reach Bethlehem. They did not know what they would meet there, but they would meet it together, with strong hearts. Strong hearts would be needed.

A few feet away, a guardian kept watch. Michael had heard everything that was said. He wasn't really listening. As a guardian, he heard the prayers of all charges he protected. And these two would need protection. He could feel the forces gathering about them, unseen. He knew they would not attack yet. He was too strong, and their master too far away. But soon now, very soon, that would change. They could afford to wait.

Michael settled down for the night. He was a guardian warrior, archangel, protector of the innocent. Tonight, no harm would come to these children. And if anyone could have been witness, they would have heard a sound as if a great parachute had just opened with a whoosh of air, followed by the sight of what appeared to be two great wings unfolding from a solitary figure, the wings so white as to be a translucent blue. This solitary figure would be sitting on a rock, upon a rise, with a large sheathed sword on his lap. You might notice a slight incandescent glow about the figure upon the rock; a brightness coming from within and around, just a hint of the power contained within. Something else you might notice, if you were very observant, is that a very similar glow came from the simple shepherd staff that, even in sleep, the boy Christopher held onto ever so tightly. Still, things look different at dusk in the desert wilderness. It could have been a trick of the light.

The next day dawned bright and hopeful. By noon, they were sharing the road with many other pilgrims anxious to see the coming event. There were shepherds, farmers, craftsmen, rich, poor, and in between from all walks of life. All had come to see the savior that would be born soon, under the new star, foretold by wise men and prophets in years past.

“Look at this!” said Mira. “It’s amazing!”

“Yes,” said Michael. “So much hope in their hearts. So many possibilities.”

“I wonder how much farther it is?” said Mira. “Maybe I’ll just run ahead and find out.”

“Mira,” warned Christopher, “We should stay together. Don’t…”

“…I’ll be back soon!” she shouted as she dashed off.

“Mira!” Christopher shouted after her as she disappeared in a sea of pilgrims. “It’ll be dark soon,” he said, an edge of fear in his voice.

"Oh, don't worry about her," said Michael, attempting to reassure the boy. "She'll be fine. Let's stop and rest for a while." He motioned Christopher to follow him to the shade of a nearby tree.

Christopher kept looking in the direction she had gone. "Do you think she'll be alright?" he asked. "Are you kidding?" said Michael. "I feel sorry for anyone who has the misfortune to tangle with Mira." Michael smiled to himself. "That girl has the beauty of a desert flower, the sting of a scorpion, and the cunning of a fox. Trust me. She'll be fine. Besides, it gives us a chance to talk. Now, once we get to Bethlehem, we may not have time to..."

"...Michael, do you know anything about women?" asked Christopher anxiously.

This was unexpected. There really wasn't time for this. "Just so that we understand each other," said Michael, "you think that because I am a soldier and have been around, I know something about women."

"Yes," said Christopher.

"You think that I am a man of the world, therefore I know of women and have known women."

Christopher said nothing. He just nodded his head up and down quickly, not unlike the batter who receives the swing-away sign from the third-base coach. Michael let out a long, heavy sigh, hands folded, looking down at the ground. Finally, he looked up at the eager face of the youthful Christopher, thirsting for universal knowledge. "My friend, you could not be farther from the truth."

"Huh?" said Christopher, visibly disappointed at his unenlightenment.

Michael gave Christopher a wry smile; part quizzical, part comical, with one eyebrow up and one down. "Yes," he said. "I have been around the camp a few times. I have been to the edges of the world and have seen many strange and wonderful things…and I am older than I look Christopher…much older." He sighed again. "You may think that I am wise in the ways of women … ."

Christopher held his breath, bit his tongue, and closed his eyes in anticipation. Finally, he would understand what he considered a great mystery. "What is this…power, this strange knowledge that they have that men lack?"

Michael simply shrugged his shoulders and said, "A woman is a mystery to me."

Christopher had nearly passed out from holding his breath. Before he could protest, Michael continued on. "She is physically weaker than a man, but her heart and spirit are strong and she endures great hardship for long periods of time. She endures; she raises the young, cares for the old, and buries the dead. She bends but does not break. The man breaks. He is strong, but he has not the resilience for the long haul without his female companion." He tapped the hilt of his sword. "The sword is strong, good for close combat, but to fight the long fight, you need a bow. The two together are formidable in battle. And yet, it is man who rules and the woman serves. It is a mystery to me."

Christopher was silent. He had never thought about the differences between men and women in these terms before. It made him think. He realized how he had taken his mother for granted.

As if reading his mind, Michael said, "It's alright, Christopher. Even the best of sons, in time, will break his mother's heart. He will grow to manhood and leave her. It is the way of things."

There was a moment of silence while the two contemplated the mystery between man and woman, mother and son. Finally, Michael broke the moment. "How do you feel about Mira?"

Christopher sat down next to Michael with a sigh. "I…I'm not sure." He stared at the ground. "I've never felt this way before. I can't seem to stop thinking about her. She is so…" He turned to Michael. "It's the best feeling I've ever had. It's better than singing…but I'm so…confused."

Michael studied Christopher's face for a moment. "Mmmm…" he said, like a doctor looking for signs of illness in a patient. "…you have the look about you."

"Huh?" said Christopher. "What look?" He had been thinking about her even now.

"That look," said Michael. "The one that says you either ate some spoiled mutton or you're in love." Michael smiled. He had seen that look many times in his existence. It was a look he never got tired of. It was one of the things that endeared these favorites of God to him: their ability to grow in the ways of love, pain, and forgiveness amazed him. *How do they do it?* he wondered to himself.…*So little time.*

Michael spoke to the ground. He didn't want to embarrass Christopher, or make him uncomfortable by facing him directly. "Do you care for her?" Christopher just looked at him. He did not answer. "If you do, then you should tell her," said Michael.

"But…but…" Christopher now had a positively panicked look on his face. "…but then she would know!"

Michael was so enjoying this conversation. He liked this boy. He had character. "And, her knowing would pose a problem?" asked Michael.

"Well, yes…she'd know!" said Christopher, as if that should be explanation enough.

Michael was confused. "Why should she not know your feelings?" he asked.

"Well…" said Christopher, "What if she doesn't feel the same?"

"Good question," said Michael. "If she does not feel the same, would you care about her any less?"

"No," said Christopher with no ambiguity.

"Then tell her," said Michael. "Tell her now." There was a quality in Michael's voice and a look on his face that said many things. Christopher understood the unspoken message: *Tell her now while there is still time.* Michael knew these two. He was gifted with the ability to see the soul as it resides within the body. The souls of Christopher and Mira were pure white without blemish. When they were together, they shone with a brightness of light born of a complimentary evolution he had seldom seen in two this young. Her strengths were his weaknesses, as his strengths were hers. Together, they were much more than they were separately. The bond between them was already strong, yet flexible, like a footbridge crossing a wide river. Oh yes, these two were meant to be; Michael could see that, which was well. For the power they would face could only be defeated by the power love creates.

"Tell her now," Michael repeated as he caught sight of her running toward them. She was having a difficult time getting to them, since she was coming in the opposite direction of the general movement of the crowd, slowly making its way to Bethlehem. Finally, out of breath, she reached them.

"Mira," said Christopher, "I need to talk..."

"Wait," she interrupted. "Christopher, Michael, I have found the child we seek." She turned to Christopher. "...right where our dreams said he would be."

Then her eyes began to tear as she looked at Michael. "...but there is someone else there, too...someone who knows you, Michael. Someone... or...something...dark."

"When I hear music, I fear no danger, I am invulnerable, I see no foe. I am related to the earliest times, and to the latest."

—HENRY DAVID THOREAU

CHAPTER 6:

PROPHESIES FULFILLED

...and the dragon stood before the woman who was ready to give birth for to devour her child as soon as it was born.

—REVELATION 12:4

It was late when they arrived. Christopher wasted no time in pushing through the crowd. He had to make sure he wasn't too late. Finally he was there, but there was one lone figure that refused to let him through.

"Excuse me..." the person in front ignored him. "Pardon me, sir..." Still, no movement. Finally, desperately wanting to see the child, he gave a gentle, but firm nudge, while raising his voice a notch. "Please, I need to see the child!"

Then he stopped and the blood left his face as he recognized this intruder. It was Belial, alias Hirsute Hairy. He smiled an evil smile with no pretense at disguise as he did when he played the part of the staff salesman. Christopher was close enough to feel the fetid breath of this inhuman being at the back of his throat. His eyes were yellow, with a vertical slit, and his teeth were large and canine. Flies buzzed around his head like vultures searching for their next meal.

"Better hurry," Belial said. "He won't be around much longer." Then he opened his mouth and laughed in Christopher's face, the primeval laugh of a hyena about to feed. Christopher thought he saw maggots crawling around in that maw.

"You!" was all he could say.

Belial, his eyes narrowing, leaned closer. "Should've given me the staff when you had the chance, boy."

Christopher was genuinely frightened now, but he refused to back down. *Don't look away,*" he kept saying to himself. Somehow, he found the strength to look Belial in the eye. "I told you," he said, "You can't have it." They held each other's gaze. It was Belial who blinked.

"No matter," he said. Now he lowered his voice to a whisper from the grave. "When my master is finished with you, you will beg him to take it." The foul breath now smelled like burning flesh and, combined with the buzzing flies, Christopher began to lose focus and spiral downward.

"What would your master take from him?" Michael, sword of the light, strongest guardian in the cosmos, now stood beside Christopher, eyes blazing blue fire at Belial. Christopher leaned against Michael gratefully. His head began to clear as the terrible smell was replaced by the gentle scent of Frankincense and Myrrh, carried on the dessert breeze.

Belial, his face twisting in one moment from glee to anger, spat at Michael. "You know, man of the sword!"

Michael was calm. He had known this confrontation was coming. He had waited for millennia. There was no reason to rush it now. "Tell me, Belial, why is your master so interested in the staff?"

"You know why, Michael. It belongs to me!" It was Lucifer.

Michael didn't seem surprised to find his old enemy there. In fact, he rather expected to. The two stared at one another. There he stood, brother, enemy, Lucifer, Satan. The adversary of whom Belial was a mere lieutenant.

"If you have harmed that child...," Michael began.

"Oh, no no. I haven't...yet," said Lucifer. "I have to wait a bit. Midnight is my hour now, Michael. It is the darkest part of the night, when my strength waxes and yours and his (he gestured toward the manger) wanes. And he is strong, Michael. I feel his strength, his purpose, even though he is only an infant." He looked toward the manger. "Oh, yes. He's got to go, that one does."

Michael was in anguish. Once again, he found himself trying to talk Lucifer out of the folly of a plan doomed to failure. "You cannot win. The child is the chosen. You must understand, Lucifer, you and I are only the messengers..." Then Michael turned toward the manger where a baby had just been born. "...He is the message."

Lucifer looked toward the manger as well and spoke the words that meant there would be no compromise. No quarter. "He must go, Michael. He must die."

"Why?" asked Michael. "Why destroy the child?"

Lucifer now looked upon Michael with a scowl that would wither an oak. "Because! He stands upon ground that belongs to me! He is a threat to me and my kingdom on Earth, and I will not have it!" Lucifer suddenly became calm and less animated. "He is the chosen. Therefore, he must die." It was presented as a fact, followed by a conclusion. Lucifer could have been a professor stating a mathematical formula.

Now, Lucifer began to soften. He placed a brotherly hand on Michael's shoulder. "Why don't you go back to the clouds, Michael? We were brothers once, created from the fire of God, that white light that no mortal eyes can bear. Why should we now bow before something made of clay?" He looked directly into Michael's eyes. "Why are you here?" He spoke with such sincerity and concern. "It has been long since your feet have felt the dust of the earth. How many hundreds of years? Perhaps since you drove the sinners from the garden."

Michael continued to look at Lucifer. Was he remembering? He might have even nodded his head slightly.

"You have always been the one that loved to fly into the sun, my brother; to soar into the storm just to follow the thunder to its source. You were always the best of us. Well, second best, anyway," he corrected. "Do not fight me, Michael. Do not dirty your hands now. It is not worth it," he whispered darkly.

Michael looked into the eyes of his wayward brother for a long time. Perhaps he was remembering a time eons past when there were no mortals to watch over, all the guardians did was fly, and not even the sky was the limit because they were the first created and first loved by God. But now Michael was back on earth with a job to do. He looked at Lucifer. There was no challenge or battle lust in his voice or his eyes when finally, he answered, "You offer me what is not yours to give, nor mine to receive."

Now, Lucifer's demeanor began to change. He scowled at Michael. "You will not find it easy to vanquish me," he said. "Perhaps you will defeat me, but I will take this earth you are so fond of with me! Leave while there is still time."

Michael now knew that this prodigal son would not return to the family. He answered simply: "I cannot."

"So be it," Lucifer answered flatly. "Excuse me," he said as he pointedly turned his back to Michael. "I have to prepare, but first…" and, with a backward wave of his hand, everyone around closed their eyes and fell into a deep sleep. Lucifer glanced over his shoulder and smiled his toothy smile. "No witnesses," he said, making the last syllable sound very much like the hiss of a snake. Now, he turned and came face to face with Christopher and Mira. "Why aren't those two asleep with the rest of the clay figures?" he asked.

Michael stepped between them. "They are under my protection," he said.

Lucifer looked at them with the eyes of a hungry wolf. "We'll see about that," he said to Michael. "Oh," he said, returning his hungry look to Christopher, "...Don't try to stop me. Tell them, Michael. And remember, you can't stop me either unless you use the sword, Sword Man." He laughed as he strutted back to the manger.

Mira was the first to snap back to reality, as surreal as it was. "Michael, what is this about??"

Michael kept his eyes on Lucifer as he walked toward the manger. "I am here for the same purpose you are; to save the child." Mira and Christopher looked at each other, then back to Michael.

Christopher tried to ask one of many questions. "But how did..."

"...... no time to explain," said Michael. "If we do not stop him, he will kill the Christ-child, the Savior that was foretold."

They heard the sound of an infant cooing. It was strange. The child did not seem in distress at all. It was as if he knew that all would be well.

"It is almost time," Lucifer said as he stepped out of the manger, holding the babe in his arms. He held him up. "The little pretender, the savior of humankind! Destroyed by the one true king: Lucifer! The enlightened one! I have many other names, you know."

He was now talking directly to the child. "My favorite is Morning Star. Do you know why, little lamb?"

The baby cooed again.

"...because the morning star refuses to stop shining. Even at dawn, as the sun's rays peek over the horizon, the star continues to twinkle brightly, as if to say; 'I am not finished! I'm still here. I choose to stay!' Even when rendered invisible by the great, clumsy, ubiquitous orb, it's still there. You just can't see it. For the sun refuses to let anything or anyone shine in its presence! But...kill the sun! Snuff it out...and the star returns."

Then Lucifer laid the child on the bare ground and, after drawing strange symbols in the dirt around the child, he withdrew from beneath his cloak two long, wicked daggers, both also with strange symbols upon the blades. He raised the black daggers, pointed them up, and crossed them while he mumbled something to himself in a strange tongue. The child only looked up at Lucifer with a curiously serene expression upon his face. He...did not cry. *Why wasn't he crying?* Lucifer looked down at the child and then quickly looked away, averting his eyes from the gaze of the child. Then it seemed his resolve returned. With a scowl, he looked up at Michael, who seemed frozen with indecision. "Say good-bye to the light, Mike," as he quickly raised the terrible weapons.

"Wait!" cried Mira. Lucifer hesitated for a moment. "Michael!" she shouted. "Are you or are you not a warrior? Stop him!"

Lucifer enjoyed what he took to be doubt in Michael's eyes. "Yes, Michael," he taunted. "Stop me! Draw the sword! Come, sword man, I dare you! Let's reach out and torch somebody! Fire the earth! Fire the universe! He'll just make another!" As he gestured toward the sky. "Will he do it in less than seven days? I wonder. Maybe he'll get it right this time!"

He placed the knife to his chin, as if thinking to himself. "What would it feel like to lose that many clay souls, all at once?"

Michael looked at him in dismay. He had indeed, lost a brother.

"He hasn't killed that many since…when…the flood? How will it feel when you draw that sword, Michael? The sword you would use to defeat me and destroy your precious Earth. Will it feel good? Come, Michael!," he continued to taunt him. "Come, Michael of the flaming sword!" He brandished his daggers. "I've learned a few tricks since my ignominious fall. What about you, Michael? Let's see what you've got!"

The wind had picked up and was whipping hair, clothes, and dust about, and where, just moments earlier, there had been peace under a shining star, now was a storm. Thunder boomed overhead and lightning lit the night, etching four silhouettes against the desertscape. There were voices in the air. Some seemed to be in anguish, begging Michael to end their pain, while others sounded like warrior angels gathering for the last great battle; he heard the drawing of swords from scabbards, arrows plucking taut bow strings, and the rattling of spears against shields. He knew the wind was created by millions of pairs of great wings as they slowed their descent from heaven, just as demons sped their ascent from hell. He lifted his eyes to heaven, hoping for a word or a sign, but there was nothing. *Why was He silent?*

Michael was in anguish. There were tears in his eyes. When had he cried last? Was it when he had been given the task of driving Adam and Eve from the Garden? Was it when he cast out Lucifer after the first battle? He had never known indecision…until now, but he did know one thing. Lucifer was on thin ice. "Demon!" he shouted in a voice that echoed off distant mountains, mixing with the distant thunder, "You, whom I once called brother! You forget your place! Do not presume to dictate the hour the sword shall be drawn!"

Christopher had not been idle during these last tense moments. He was listening to both Lucifer and Michael, and was finally beginning to put together the pieces. Lucifer, Michael, the birth of the Savior, and his staff all tied together. Mira had already guessed a few things of her own. She turned to Christopher just as he called her name. Well, she didn't exactly turn just toward Christopher. It was his staff she was looking at. She remembered now the strange power he had over the animals when he sang.

"Mira!" Christopher shouted over the wind, "I think I know what is happening!"

"Good!" she said, "because I don't think we have much time! Look!" She shouted as she pointed up.

Christopher gasped as his knees buckled. In the heavens were thousands, no, millions of winged figures, coming to earth in a great spiral. He could not see details or faces, only silhouettes against the bright sky when the lightning flashed. They appeared to be drawing up ranks, as if in preparation for battle.

Christopher rose from his knees and met Mira as she ran to him. Even though right next each other, they still had to scream over the howling wind…or was that something else?

"I think I know what must be done!" Christopher shouted.

"Then do it now, Christopher!" she shouted, desperation in her voice. "We're out of time!"

The howl of the wind was not the only sound they heard. There was something else; an unholy sound, like the lust of demons that smelled blood. Christopher tried to concentrate, but the voices in the air were confusing him, muddling his mind. He looked to Mira. "I can't!" He could barely form the words he wanted to say in his mind, much less speak them. "More time!" was all he could manage.

Mira, however, was not confused, and when she spoke to Christopher, he understood her well. There was a calm in her voice, like a breeze on the ocean, and the look of cold, steel-hard determination in her eyes when she said, "I know what I must do." She then took his face between her hands and held his eyes with hers for a moment. And within that brief island of peace, the wind and voices momentarily subsided. For no demon howl can be heard over the power of love. Much passed between them in that moment, but no words were spoken. Then, they kissed, just briefly. There was no awkwardness. It felt right. Now she turned and marched directly toward Lucifer.

"Wait!" Christopher shouted. "What are you doing?" Then the realization of what she was doing crashed in upon him.

"Buying time," she said without breaking stride or looking back.

Lucifer, having been rebuffed by Michael on the drawing of the sword, had wasted no time in returning to the task at hand. "Pity," was all he said to Michael's refusal to fight. Then, bringing the killing blades high above the child and speaking arcane words that seemed to weave symbols and runes into the very air, he reached a climax, paused, closed his eyes, and plunged down the knives. Imagine his surprise when he looked down at the last instant to see Mira covering the body of the child with her own. She had just wanted to get the child away, but then she saw the knives. She followed her instincts. Save the child…

"Noooooo!" cried Christopher as he rushed to her. He cradled her in his arms and gently rocked her back and forth, speaking to her quietly through tears, as if trying to coax the departed spirit back to her body. Now, the baby began to cry. But this was not the caustic wail that parents and siblings are accustomed to when the infant needs milk, or changing, or burping. This was the gentle flow of tears of grief for a pure and strong departed soul, the first of many to be called for His sake.

Michael saw it all. In his warrior's existence he had seen many selfless acts of courage that rated heaven's embrace, but for one so young to give her life so willingly…somehow this act touched a part of him seldom touched…and Michael wept.

It seemed that all around him, it was the same. A moment of silence was observed by the howling wind and the roaring thunder. The Earth seemed to slow its revolution, and all became strangely quiet and still. Michael knelt beside Christopher and placed a hand on his shoulder. "Christopher, you must listen to me. We do not have time to grieve."

Christopher wiped the tears from his eyes and looked up at Michael expectantly. "Listen to me, Christopher, and know that I speak the truth. I am Michael, First Archangel of the Light. I was created second by God. Lucifer was first. He stood against us in the first battle for heaven and was defeated. He hates me because I humbled him and cast him out. He hates you because you have a talisman of power that he thinks belongs to him, as well as a human soul, which is pure and incorruptible, and closer to God than he will ever be. Now he has come to Earth, and he will take revenge on humanity and heaven by making the Earth his. He has slain Mira and he will slay the child, who is the Savior that was foretold."

Christopher wiped another tear from his eye and looked at Michael. "But…" he stammered, "you…you have a sword…"

"Yes," said Michael. "My sword can destroy him, but if drawn, will also bring the end of the world."

Christopher blinked his eyes and shook his head. "I don't understand," he said.

Michael continued with the explanation. "At the end of the first battle in heaven, it was prophesied that the next time the sword is drawn, that would be the end of the world; 'When next the flaming sword is drawn, that will be the earth's last dawn.'"

Christopher's eyes widened. "That's right," said Michael. "...the apocalypse; the day of judgment. It is not time for that, Christopher. Not yet."

"But, what can I do?" asked Christopher.

"There is something you can do," replied Michael. "Something only you can do as the one who bears the talisman. Lucifer can be defeated, but it requires a sacrifice; one only you can make."

"What is this sacrifice?" asked Christopher.

Michael hesitated. "To wield such power, you must pay a price."

Christopher thought of Mira and her sacrifice. He knew he could do no less. "Tell me what to do, Michael..." He looked down at Mira. He would grieve later. He looked back up to Michael. "...and I will do it." There was no hesitation in Christopher now. His mind was clear. He would stop Lucifer or die trying.

Michael sighed heavily. "The die is cast," he said, "and I know not which way it will turn. Already, events have happened differently than I foresaw. Perhaps I was not meant to defeat the beast, for that is what he has become and no longer the brother I once loved." He paused again as if comprehending the meaning of his own words. "Very well. We must have faith." He glanced up at Lucifer and then back to Christopher. "A distraction will be needed..." and Michael explained his plan to Christopher while time slowed and the heavens waited and suspense hung thick in the aether.

As if on cue after hearing Christopher and Michael's plan, the baby broke out in a wail and the thunder, wind, and lightening returned.

Amid the chaos, Lucifer screamed, "Leave the boy to me, Michael! If he knew how to use the staff, he'd have done so by now! Your plans have failed. Only you can stop me! You and the sword! Tell me, should I make the parents watch the murder of their child or kill them first? No matter to you! You'll watch them all die!" He took off his cloak to reveal the monstrous wings Chris had first seen in his dream and, even now was still observing as an innocent bystander. Lucifer looked infinitely more menacing now, and Michael diminished in size and majesty. "… cause you haven't got the guts to use that sword. You're impotent! God's warrior…" Then he spat in disgust. "Guess what they say is true, Michael. If you don't use it, you lose it!"

"Enough!" cried Michael.

Lucifer was enjoying the game of taunting his rival. He owed him for defeating him and casting him out. It was payback time. "Oh Michael, what will you do? Are you going to sing to me? Are you going to bring back the music? Show me, Michael! Show me what you will do! I haven't got all night!"

Lucifer didn't have to wait long for a response.

"You want battle, Satan? You shall have your wish!" The name Satan echoed into the distance and was lost in the storm. It was the first time Lucifer had been called that name, and its meaning was not lost on him: Satan, the adversary. Now Michael removed the sword and scabbard, which seemed to be pulsating with light. Michael did not reveal his wings. For now, his feet would remain firmly connected to mother Earth. Screaming in rage, he lifted the sword and scabbard high above his head. It began to rain in sheets, with a corresponding increase in the rest of the storm. It seemed the wail of the child was part of the very air itself. With the weapon above his head, Michael began to draw the sword from the scabbard. Christopher looked up and sucked in air. The sword was on fire.

Michael held on tight, the muscles in his arms and shoulders trembling with effort. It was as if the sword had a mind of its own and was not ready to come out yet. It seemed it was actually fighting to get back into the scabbard. Lucifer's attention was fully on Michael, now. He was finally going to get his re-match. Everything else could wait.

Now, it was Christopher's time to fulfill his part of the plan. The sword was halfway out. Christopher felt the ground begin to shake beneath his feet. He took up his staff and began to perform the required ritual. The staff began to pulsate with a silver-white glow, but not exactly the same as Michael's sword. *So,* Christopher thought to himself fleetingly, *The sword and the staff are both talismans of power, as Michael said.* He glanced over at Michael, who seemed to be the eye of his own private hurricane as the wind whipped around him in a circle. The tremors beneath were getting more intense. Not much time left. Lucifer was completely distracted now, with two long wicked blades in his hands, waiting. This would be a fight to the death, if that were possible between two archangels.

The fiery sword was almost completely out of the scabbard now, the wind a screaming banshee, the ground shaking, causing rocks and pebbles to dance around as if they had a life of their own. It was time. Christopher, having finished the prescribed ritual, rose with the staff, twirling it above his head three times like a drum major. It felt like the right thing to do, and as he did so the silver-white pulsations increased. After the third circle was made in the air, he brought it down to the ground, hard. There was a loud thunderclap as air, wind, rain, earth and fire climaxed. Then silence. All noise—wind, rain, quaking of earth—stopped. There was utter quiet as twigs and leaves settled to the ground. Michael smiled and slammed the sword, now without pulsations or fire, back into the scabbard. Now was the time. Lucifer turned from Michael to the source of the silence. All eyes were on Christopher and his staff. The stage was set.

Christopher looked up to the stars, which had returned. He knew the warrior angels were still there; they only waited. Christopher began to sing in his high, lilting tenor voice, a melody born of pain and grief and the promise of redemption. He and the staff became one as grace flowed from his song and the earth listened. It was only a verse, the same verse he sang to his charges every night, but it resonated to all who would listen. "Little lamb, do not cry. Do not worry, for I am here. I will send the wolf away, keep the jackals all at bay. Oh, little lamb, do not fear." And the baby, Jesus, smiled.

"Oh dear," said Lucifer sarcastically, "…someone's been practicing! No matter, I will deal with you in a moment." He took a step toward the child, intending to take care of business before the situation got out of hand. Things were not going as planned. He raised the knives. "

Satan!" The voice, which moments ago was merely human, was human no longer. It was amplified many times. It contained power; a power that was not there before.

Lucifer turned toward the voice. The boy stood facing him. There was no fear in him now. His voice was calm, and there was a faint, but perceptible, glow about him. Something had happened. There was now a hint of something in Lucifer's voice as he spoke. Maybe not fear, but definitely hesitation. This was not at all going as planned.

"You dare to address me in such a manner?!" said Lucifer haughtily. "I am…"

"A liar! Thief! Kin slayer!" cried Christopher in his new voice. Now, he quietly lowered the staff and pointed it at Lucifer. "Step away from that child, now." The final word, *now* was emphasized enough to carry with it a palpable threat.

As if to test the boy, Lucifer took another step toward the child. Then another. Christopher wasted no time. He lifted the staff high above his head and brought the end of the staff down hard as another clap of thunder sounded while shards of electricity raced along the length of the staff, spilling to the ground. Lucifer backed away from the child, holding his ears as a low bass note began to emanate from the staff to the ground outward. Now, having given the downbeat, Christopher began to count measures as the sounds increased, vibrating the very air itself, the storm raging in harmony with the sound; wind and rain helping build a gigantic chord; thunder and lightening pounding out the percussion. Christopher counted slowly from the initial thunderclap down beat. With the second beat, he shifted the staff to the right while the end of the staff remained firmly planted in the ground. With the third beat, the staff shifted left as the sound gained in strength and momentum. On the fourth beat, he picked up the staff in preparation for starting another measure and brought the downbeat hard to the ground for another thunderclap. He counted four slow measures like this, all the while summoning power. Chris was amazed at the image he saw. Christopher was directing the storm as if he was a drum major on the parade field. *Awesome*, he thought to himself.

As the storm of sound grew, Christopher could be heard "By the power of the heavenly hosts!" he began. "By the power of the sacred music that was lost and is found, I summon the angels!" Thunder was now no longer necessary. The voice of Christopher was thunder. Lightning bolts began to strike the staff as the power continued to build. "Seraphim! Cherubim! Princes, and Powers! Come to me!" Now, a great cacophony of sound could be heard in addition to the storm, building a gigantic major musical chord. Horns, trumpets, drums, voices by the hundreds of thousands, perhaps millions, joined in as one voice The very cosmos seemed to be breaking out in a song of sympathetic vibration, with every star in the heavens singing of joy, peace on Earth, good will toward all men.

Christopher kept on. He was glowing now, almost transparent. He summoned the archangels. "Gabriel! Raphael! Uriel! Michael! I call you to battle!" The music, like a great bird of prey in chains, strained to break its earthly bonds, stretching the chain, straining toward sun and stars, the tension unbearable…almost…and with a wave of his staff, just before the final chord that would forever free the music, Christopher cut off the cacophony completely and left the tension hanging in the air along with the staff, glowing with an unearthly white light.

Silence. Complete and total. Nothing stirred. Christopher now possessed the full power of the talisman. He literally controlled the music of the cosmos, which was given by God and stolen by Lucifer. Now, he was ready to deal, and he hoped his adversary was also.

"You have lost this battle," he said to Lucifer. "Leave this place, now…" and an ever-so-faint smile played across his face, with one eyebrow up and one down, "…or face the music."

Lucifer was daunted, but he was certainly not yet defeated. He was still, after all, Lucifer. He laughed. "Whom do you think you are speaking to?" he asked. "I was created first and best by the Light of Lights! A light so great that it would incinerate you before you could look upon it. I created that which you hold in your puny, pathetic, human hands. I know its power!" He circled Christopher like a hungry hyena looking for a weakness in his potential prey. "I know the power of this talisman. Does it burn, human?" He moved closer. "Is it painful to the touch? Fool! That is because it was not meant for the touch of mortal flesh. It was meant to be wielded by the most powerful angel in Heaven and Earth! Lucifer! You are strong, boy, but you are only…" he spat, "…human, clay! Not fire! If you finish the song, use the full power of the staff, you will die. Then I will kill the child, the angels will fly away (he made a comical flapping motion with his hands)...the Earth will be mine, and I will have everything I want. If you do not use the staff, I will kill you myself. Then I will kill the child, the angels will fly away, and again, I will have everything I want!" He paused, never taking his eyes off Christopher, sizing him up, wearing him down. Now, the counter offer. "Or," he said, like the great orator making his final point. "Or, you can give the staff to me. It is a burden, is it not?"

He sounded so sympathetic. "...and, it will kill you, make no mistake. It has already taken years off your young life. What a pity. Did my brother Michael tell you that? I...think not," he said with a sideways glance at Michael. Christopher said nothing. Lucifer continued, "If you give me the staff, I can reward you. Riches beyond your imagination, power undreamed of. Anything, anything you want. Think, boy. Whatever you choose, I win. I get everything I want. Why shouldn't you have something for your trouble? After all, you're just human." He paused again. "Now, I've a child to kill, angels to disperse, and a world to rule. I'm behind schedule. Tell me your answer, boy."

Christopher looked at Michael. Michael merely nodded to him. *Go on,* he seemed to say. *It's out of my hands.* Christopher looked up and then all around. He was feeling very tired from the effects of the staff. That was the human side of him. But there was another part of him, an aspect he barely recognized, but still knew. And that part of him was ready.

It seemed like the whole world was holding its breath, waiting for him to decide. He was so tired. He just wanted to get this over with. Finally, he turned to face Lucifer. "I may be just human, but I have something which you do not, something more precious even than this staff. It is something you have never had in all the time you've existed." His strength failing, Christopher raised the staff high above his head.

"It is a treasure you will never possess no matter how hard you try." The staff began to glow and radiate heat. "...No matter who you kill." A low hum had started, and was increasing in pitch and volume. "This treasure belongs to me and me alone." He stirred the air with the end of the staff. Lucifer began to doubt. Faster and faster, the staff turned until it seemed alive, creating a whirlwind of light, a perfect funnel cloud of light and sound that led to the hand of the conductor, the rhythm master. "This treasure, which belongs only to me, is forbidden to you." Lucifer began to back away slowly. So fast did the staff turn now that it was like the blur of a hummingbird wing; the tone, joined by other tones, continued to climb in pitch and volume, the elements vibrating in sympathy.

"And what is this treasure?" Lucifer asked sarcastically.

"My soul," Christopher replied and, with that, he plunged the staff deep into the earth, completing the cycle.

From its source, the light spread across the ground, across the rocks, trees, mountain ranges, and oceans. Christopher sang, the same song he always sang when his charges were frightened. But now he sang to a frightened child, wanting only what every child wants: to be safe from the darkness, to be loved.

Little lamb, do not cry. Do not worry, I am here. I will send the wolf away Keep the jackals all at bay. Little lamb, do not fear.

At the same moment the light flew into the air like a bomb burst to heaven; a million iridescent doves spreading from a single source on earth to myriad sources in space.

Stop all your worries. They shall not last. Leave all of your bad dreams behind. Let them come for thee. They shall not pass while I stand with my staff by your side.

In that instant, ten-thousand-thousand voices and ten-thousand-thousand instruments began to sing and play a song of joy.

Little Lamb don't shed a tear. All you need is here with me. So close your eyes and breathe deep sighs, and I will watch over thee, and I will watch over thee.

The music had been returned and the hosts of heaven, armed not with sword, bow, and spear, but with voice, drum, and horn, drove away the darkness, fulfilling the prophecy that was foretold: That on that night, the Savior would be born, and the Music returned.

Lucifer, who measured all men only by his standards of greed and lust for power, never expected Christopher to commit the ultimate sacrifice of giving up his life that another may live. He pressed his hands against his ears in agony, for this music was anathema to him, utter defeat.

"Music is nature's love and tears transformed into harmonies that reach the spirit of man."

—DORA FLICK-FLOOD

CHAPTER 7:

GREETINGS, FAREWELLS, AND GREETINGS

Christopher was nowhere to be seen, and his body was never found. Perhaps he was made a part of the light he created through his conduction of the sacred symphony of sound back to heaven and earth. As a human lightning rod for angelic power, he happily paid the ultimate price, gave the greatest gift.

Lucifer, still holding his ears, rose from his knees and began to fade. He wasn't about to hang around. He had lost this battle, but the outcome of the war was still undecided. He was almost gone when Michael stepped out of the shadows.

"Hold, demon!" he shouted. Lucifer immediately rematerialized, a scowl on his face.

"This isn't over, Michael," he said. "I'll be back, again and again!"

"I know," said Michael. "…and I'll be waiting, with a smile on my face and a song in my heart, thanks to Christopher. But before you leave…" Michael took off his cloak. As he loosened the sword and scabbard, Michael's two huge wings appeared on his shoulders. Now, it was Lucifer's turn to take his medicine. Michael placed the sword before him point down and laid his hands upon the hilts. The sword and scabbard began to glow. A low, intense tone, faint yet strong, could be heard as many invisible pairs of eyes looked on. Then Michael pronounced the doom of Lucifer: "Brother you once were to me; now, no longer, for I see that you are beyond redemption. Your name shall be Satan, the Adversary, from now till the end of days. And since you have chosen the ways of the beast, you shall become the beast."

Lucifer dropped to one knee. Something terrible was happening. He had always been proud of his appearance, being very vain. Now, that appearance was changing. First, his lower body changed from human form to that of a goat. His legs grew thick, matted hair and his feet were transformed into cloven hooves. It is a difficult task to stand upright with the legs and feet of a goat, but Satan refused to go down on his knees, a position of penitence. From then on, he would be in extreme pain as a result of this anatomical anomaly. Quickly, his hands went up to his temples and he howled in pain as from between his fingers sprouted horns, along with profuse amounts of blood. His shiny white smile became large, misshapen fangs with poisonous saliva dripping from them. His wings sprang from his shoulders and, as they spread to take flight, the beautiful blue-black feathers molted from them and were replaced by skin stretched across long, bony fingers; bat wings from which such a stench arose that it made even Satan retch.

"This, then is your punishment," pronounced Michael. "That you shall go about the earth thus, that man shall know that you are, indeed, the beast, until you repent your ways, or…the end of the world. Now, get thee gone!" There was an explosion of fire and smoke with a scream of anger and despair, then, nothing but the night.

Michael was alone now except for the child, still lying on the ground, looking up at him. "Welcome, little lamb," he said as he picked up the child. He then returned him to the manger. By the time the sleep had cleared from everyone's eyes, Michael was well out of sight and back to where the confrontation had taken place. He knelt beside the body of Mira and had just leaned down to brush the hair from her face when his angel senses told him to be alert, for another of his kind was near.

"Christopher? Is that you?" Michael called in no direction in particular. From high up upon a rocky out-cropping came his answer.

"Here, Michael," said Christopher as he stepped down from the rocks.

Michael embraced Christopher warmly. "Welcome to the Light," Michael said.

"Thanks," said Christopher. Then he saw Mira. He walked over to her and again cradled her in his arms. Michael knelt beside him with a hand on his shoulder. "It wasn't her time," said Christopher.

"Yes, I know," said Michael. "Your fate was written in the book. Hers was not. Not yet."

"What does that mean?" asked Christopher.

"It means," sighed Michael, "that she still had some living to do; perhaps a destiny to fulfill. We'll have to bring her back. There are rules that must be followed; lines that must be allowed to continue to their logical end."

"Huh?" asked Christopher.

Michael ignored him. "Take my hand," he said. "Now, hold her." With his other hand, Michael now took Mira's free hand. The three completed a circle, with Mira between the two angels. "Close your eyes," said Michael. "Concentrate on Mira, and don't let anything distract you." They both closed their eyes, and Christopher did what Michael said. Soon, Christopher felt warmth coursing through him and a strange feeling of lightness. Without thinking, he just barely opened one eye.

He closed it immediately because he didn't want what he saw to break his concentration.

What he had seen was not one, but two pairs of wings surrounding the three of them in a circle of light. One pair of wings belonged to Michael. The other pair, not quite as full as Michael's, was somehow attached to his own shoulders. Beyond the sphere of light they formed were many hundreds of other wings attached to the shoulders of angels, all glowing with the same soft light, forming concentric circles around the circle of three on the ground and spiraling upward. And, as tears came to Christopher's eyes, they began to sing. He could not quite make out the words, but it really didn't matter. The message was conveyed through the music as clearly as if they sang directly to him. It started low and began to build, layer upon layer of tones, harmonies, and melodies, which wove into and out of each other in a symphonic tapestry of hope, love, grace, and redemption. And for one brief moment, Christopher thought he felt the touch of God upon his shoulder. In that moment, Christopher knew many things: forgiveness, that unconditional love that can only come from God, new beginnings, and, above all, the first Christmas. Christopher looked down. As he did, a tear from his cheek fell upon Mira's forehead. Her chest began to move up and down. She was breathing.

"Mira," he said softly. Her eyes fluttered and opened. Her wounds were healed.

She smiled up at Christopher and Michael. "They said I have to come back for awhile," she said casually.

"Who?" asked Christopher?

"The voices…the voices in the light," she said softly. "It was so beautiful," she said as she wiped a tear from her eye. "So much love." She stood up and shook herself as if coming out of a dream. She looked at Christopher, gazing deeply into his eyes. Something was different. "You're one of them. You are of The Light now."

Christopher nodded. "The staff was not meant for human hands," he said, as if that explained everything. "The child is safe."

Mira hugged him fiercely, burying her head in his chest. "But I don't want you to be an angel!" she cried. "Not yet. I want you to stay here with me." Christopher held Mira tightly as he looked at Michael and asked a question with his eyes.

"Alright," said Michael, "...but quickly. We must leave soon." Christopher concentrated on holding Mira for a moment. He knew this hug would have to last him a long time. "Mira, I have to go." Before she could protest, he continued, "Now listen. I have some things to tell you, things that might make you feel better."

She looked up at him, questions in her eyes. "First, I promise that you and I will be together, someday. And you..." He looked at her long and hard, as if memorizing every aspect of her face. "...you will live, and grow, and be more beautiful than you are..." This was much harder than he thought it would be. "...and you will have children. And you and they will be warm and safe, and taken care of, and...watched over." Mira looked up at Christopher again. There seemed to be a faint glow about him now, a certain transparency of light and spirit. She placed a hand on his face as if to make sure he wasn't already fading away.

"How do you know these things?" she asked through tears. Christopher glanced one more time at Michael, who nodded his head. Christopher looked at Mira and reached up to take her hand, still upon his face, and wrapped his fingers around it. "Because I will be your guardian angel. And I'm not going to let anything happen to you." They embraced once more, and Christopher thought his heart would break.

Then he kissed her on the cheek. He gave the staff to Mira. It was singed on the top, but otherwise whole. "Remember me," he said.

"I will," she smiled with tears in her eyes. And then he was gone.

Somewhere high above the earth among millions of stars, amid a wondrous musical celebration for the birth of baby Jesus, Christopher felt a hand upon his shoulder. It was Michael. "I have learned a lesson from you, Christopher, and I wanted to thank you."

"A lesson?" said Christopher, "from me?"

Michael continued, "I thought it was the task of Michael to bring down the demon, but it was yours, and I was not sure you would be able to complete it. I doubted. I lacked faith because you were not a warrior... strong, like me. I had not the faith nor the humility, even though I stood in the presence of a child who, even with his humble beginnings, is destined to change the face of the earth."

He paused for a moment. "You see, Christopher, I am immortal. I cannot die. I will never be faced with the choice you made this night, whether to give up my life or no. Through your example, the angels have learned that there are many kinds of strength from which to draw, less evident they may be, but no less powerful. Perhaps that is why the souls of men and women are so close to God and why we feel such terrible grief and emptiness when they are lost to us." He turned his thought back to Christopher and, once again, Christopher felt a hand on his shoulder. "It is a valuable lesson," said Michael, "...and it is well taught."

Chris kept hearing a constant ringing in his ears, some kind of bell, nothing like he ever heard in the desert before...wait a minute. He opened his eyes as the bell rang again: doorbell! It was the doorbell! He sat up and looked around. He was in his bed, in his room. Nothing had changed. So why did he expect to be in the desert? *Ding-dong*, there went the doorbell again. *Whoa,* he said to himself, *That was a bizarre dream.*

He threw on clothes and ran to the front door. He opened the door and came face to face with the girl of his dreams. No, actually, it was the girl in his dreams. Before the shock could even register, she began talking.

"Hi," the girl said. She even sounded like Mira. "I'm putting a band together for the city parks and rec talent show. There's a cash prize. I need a drummer; you interested?"

Chris just stared and made a sound like "Uhhhhmm..." The girl's hands went to her hips.

"Uhhhm...what?" she asked, rather sarcastically. "You are the drummer, right?"

Chris began to snap out of it. *Might as well play along.* "Uhmmm, yeah, sure ... I'm interested."

"Good," she said in a no-nonsense tone.

"My name is Mary Isadora Rose Attwood ." He shook her hand and winced at her strong grip. "Wow, that's a long name," he said.

"I'm Catholic," she shot back. "You gotta problem with that ?"

"Uhhh, no, no problem."

"Good," she replied. "What's your name?"

"Chris," he said. "Just Chris ."

"Nice to meet you, Just Chris," she said. Then she smiled. "You should get that Uhhh...thing taken care of. I hope you don't start every sentence like that."

She was leading him back into his own living room by the elbow... "By the way, do you sing any?" Before he could answer, she stopped short and looked at him. "Have we met before?" she asked. They were now standing between the coffee table and the couch. Chris was about to feel very uncomfortable when something caught his eye. He glanced down at one of the pillows on the couch. Underneath, he could see the shape of an unusually large pure white feather. It was almost as if it had been left there on purpose. He looked at the girl. Later, he would realize that if you take the first letters of Mary Isadora Rose Attwood and put them together, you get MIRA.

"Uhmmm...," he said, "...that depends; do you believe in angels ?"

The girl looked at him. "Well," she said, "I am Catholic." She sat on the couch and looked up. "You're a little strange, even for a drummer."

The End...(Not)